GUNS OF THE MOUNTAINS

BY

ROBERT E. HOWARD

British Library Cataloguing-in-Publication Data
A catalogue record for this book is available from the
British Library

Robert E. Howard

Robert Ervin Howard was born in Peaster, Texas in 1906. During his youth, his family moved between a variety of Texan boomtowns, and Howard – a bookish and somewhat introverted child – was steeped in the violent myths and legends of the Old South. Although he loved reading and learning, Howard developed a distinctly Texan, hardboiled outlook on the world. He became a passionate fan of boxing, taking it up at an amateur level, and from the age of nine began to write adventure tales of semi-historical bloodshed. In 1919, when Howard was thirteen, his family moved to the Central Texas hamlet of Cross Plains, where he would stay for the rest of his life.

At fifteen Howard began to read the pulp magazines of the day, and to write more seriously. The December 1922 issue of his high school newspaper featured two of his stories, 'Golden Hope Christmas' and 'West is West'. In 1924 he sold his first piece – a short caveman tale titled 'Spear and Fang' – for $16 to the not-yet-famous *Weird Tales* magazine. He published with the magazine regularly over the next few years. 1929 was a breakout year for Howard, in that the 23-year-old writer began to sell to other magazines, such as *Ghost Stories* and *Argosy*, both of whom had previously sent him hundreds of rejection slips. In 1930, he began a correspondence with weird fiction master H. P. Lovecraft which ran up to his death six years later, and is regarded as one of the great correspondence cycles in all of fantasy literature.

It was partly due to Lovecraft's encouragement that Howard created his most famous character, Conan the Cimmerian. Conan – a barbarian-turned-King during the Hyborian Age, a mythical period of some 12,000 years ago – featured in seventeen *Weird Tales* stories between 1933 and 1936, and is now regarded as having spawned the 'sword and sorcery' genre, making Howard's influence on fantasy literature comparable to that of J. R. R. Tolkien's. The Conan stories have since been adapted many times, most famously in the series of films starring Arnold Schwarzenegger.

Howard was enjoying an all-time high in sales by the beginning of 1936, but he was also deeply upset by the ill health of his mother, who had fallen into a coma. On the morning of June 11, 1936, he asked an attending nurse whether she would ever recover, and the nurse replied negatively. Howard walked to his car, parked outside the family home in Cross Plains, and shot himself. He died eight hours later, aged just thirty.

This business begun with Uncle Garfield Elkins coming up from Texas to visit us. Between Grizzly Run and Chawed Ear the stage got held up by some masked bandits, and Uncle Garfield, never being able to forget that he was a gun-fighting fool thirty or forty years ago, pulled his old cap-and-ball instead of putting up his hands like he was advised to. For some reason, instead of blowing out his light, they merely busted him over the head with a .45 barrel, and when he come to he was rattling on his way toward Chawed Ear with the other passengers, minus his money and watch.

It was his watch what caused the trouble. That there timepiece had been his grandpap's, and Uncle Garfield sot more store by it than he did all his kin folks.

When he arriv up in the Humbolt mountains where our cabin was, he imejitly let in to howling his woes to the stars like a wolf with the belly-ache. And from then on we heered nothing but that watch. I'd saw it and thunk very little of it. It was big as my fist, and wound up with a key which Uncle Garfield was always losing and looking for. But it was solid gold, and he called it a hairloom, whatever them things is. And he nigh driv the family crazy.

"A passle of big hulks like you-all settin' around and lettin' a old man get robbed of all his property," he would say bitterly. "When I was a young buck, if'n my uncle had been abused that way, I'd of took the trail and never slept nor et till I brung back his watch and the scalp of the skunk which stole it. Men now days--" And so on and so on, till I felt like drownding the old jassack in a barrel of corn licker.

Finally pap says to me, combing his beard with his fingers: "Breckinridge," says he, "I've endured Uncle Garfield's belly-achin' all I aim to. I want you to go look for his cussed watch, and don't come back without it."

"How'm I goin' to know where to look?" I protested, aghast. "The feller which got it may be in Californy or Mexico by now."

"I realizes the difficulties," says pap. "But if Uncle Garfield knows somebody is out lookin' for his dern timepiece, maybe he'll give the rest of us some peace. You git goin', and if you can't find that watch, don't come back till after Uncle Garfield has went home."

"How long is he goin' to stay?" I demanded.

"Well," said pap, "Uncle Garfield's visits allus lasts a year, at least."

At this I bust into profanity.

I said: "I got to stay away from home a year? Dang it, pap, Jim Braxton'll steal Ellen Reynolds away from me whilst I'm gone. I been courtin' that girl till I'm ready to fall dead. I done licked her old man three times, and now, just when I got her lookin' my way, you tells me I got to up and leave her for a year for that dern Jim Braxton to have no competition with."

"You got to choose between Ellen Reynolds, and yore own flesh and blood," said pap. "I'm darned if I'll listen to Uncle Garfield's squawks any longer. You make yore own choice--but, if you don't choose to do what I asks you to, I'll fill yore hide with buckshot every time I see you from now on."

Well, the result was that I was presently riding morosely away from home and Ellen Reynolds, and in the general direction of where Uncle Garfield's blasted watch might possibly be.

I passed by the Braxton cabin with the intention of dropping Jim a warning about his actions whilst I was gone, but he wasn't there. So I issued a general defiance to the family by slinging a .45 slug through the winder which knocked a cob pipe outa old man Braxton's mouth. That soothed me a little, but I knowed very well that Jim would make a bee-line for the Reynolds' cabin the second I was out of sight. I could just see him gorging on Ellen's bear meat and honey, and bragging on hisself. I hoped Ellen would notice the difference between a loud mouthed boaster like him, and a quiet, modest young man like me, which never bragged, though admittedly the biggest man and the best fighter in the Humbolts.

I hoped to meet Jim somewhere in the woods as I rode down the trail, for I was intending to do something to kinda impede his courting while I was gone, like breaking his leg, or something, but luck wasn't with me.

I headed in the general direction of Chawed Ear, and the next day seen me riding in gloomy grandeur through a country quite some distance from Ellen Reynolds.

PAP ALWAYS SAID MY curiosity would be the ruination of me some day, but I never could listen to guns popping up in the mountains without wanting to find out who was killing who. So that morning, when I heard the rifles talking off amongst the trees, I turned Cap'n Kidd aside and left the trail and rode in the direction of the noise.

A dim path wound up through the big boulders and bushes, and the shooting kept getting louder. Purty soon I come out into a glade, and just as I did, bam! somebody let go at me from the bushes and a .45-70 slug cut both my bridle reins nearly in half. I instantly returned the shot with my .45, getting just a glimpse of something in the brush, and a man let out a squall and jumped out into the open, wringing his hands. My bullet had hit the lock of his Winchester and mighty nigh jarred his hands off him.

"Cease that ungodly noise," I said sternly, p'inting my .45 at his bay-winder, "and tell me how come you waylays innercent travelers."

He quit working his fingers and moaning, and he said: "I thought you was Joel Cairn, the outlaw. You're about his size."

"Well, I ain't," I said. "I'm Breckinridge Elkins, from the Humbolts. I was just ridin' over to learn what all the shootin' was about."

The guns was firing in the trees behind the fellow, and somebody yelled what was the matter.

"Ain't nothin' the matter," he hollered back. "Just a misunderstandin'." And he said to me: "I'm glad to see you, Elkins. We need a man like you. I'm Sheriff Dick Hopkins, from Grizzly Run."

"Where at's your star?" I inquired.

"I lost it in the bresh." he said. "Me and my deputies have been chasin' Tarantula Bixby and his gang for a day and a night, and we got 'em cornered over there in a old deserted cabin in a holler. The boys is shootin' at 'em now. I heard you comin' up the trail and snuck over to see who it is. Just as I said, I thought you was Cairn. Come on with me. You can help us."

"I ain't no deputy," I said. "I got nothin' against Tranchler Bixby."

"Well, you want to uphold the law, don't you?" he said.

"Naw," I said.

"Well, gee whiz!" he wailed. "If you ain't a hell of a citizen! The country's goin' to the dogs. What chance has a honest man got?"

"Aw, shut up," I said. "I'll go over and see the fun, anyhow."

So he picked up his gun, and I tied Cap'n Kidd, and follered the sheriff through the trees till we come to some rocks, and there was four men laying behind them rocks and shooting down into a hollow. The hill sloped away mighty steep into a small basin that was just like a bowl, with a rim of slopes all around. In the middle of this bowl there was a cabin and puffs of smoke was coming from the cracks between the logs.

The men behind the rocks looked at me in surprize, and one of them said, "What the hell--?"

But the sheriff scowled at them and said, "Boys, this here is Breck Elkins. I done told him already about us bein' a posse from Grizzly Run, and about how we got Tarantula Bixby and two of his cutthroats trapped in that there cabin."

One of the deputies bust into a guffaw and Hopkins glared at him and said: "What you laughin' about, you spotted hyener?"

"I swallered my tobaccer and that allus gives me the hystericals," mumbled the deputy, looking the other way.

"Hold up your right hand, Elkins," requested Hopkins, so I done so, wondering what for, and he said: "Does you swear to tell the truth, the whole truth and nothing but the truth, e pluribus unum, anno dominecker, to wit in status quo?"

"What the hell are you talkin' about?" I demanded.

"Them which God has j'ined asunder let no man put together," said Hopkins. "Whatever you say will be used against you and the Lord have mercy on yore soul. That means you're a deputy. I just swore you in."

"Go set on a tack," I snorted disgustedly. "Go catch your own thieves. And don't look at me like that. I might bend a gun over your skull."

"But Elkins," pleaded Hopkins, "with yore help we can catch them rats easy. All you got to do is lay up here behind this big rock and shoot at the cabin and keep 'em occupied till we can sneak around and rush 'em from the rear. See, the bresh comes down purty close to the foot of the slope on the other side, and gives us cover. We can do it easy, with somebody keepin' their attention over here. I'll give you part of the reward."

"I don't want no derned blood-money," I said, backing away. "And besides--ow!"

I'd absent-mindedly backed out from behind the big rock where I'd been standing, and a .30-30 slug burned its way acrost the seat of my britches.

"Dern them murderers!" I bellered, seeing red. "Gimme a rifle! I'll learn 'em to shoot a man behind his back. Gwan, take 'em in the rear. I'll keep 'em busy."

"Good boy!" said Hopkins. "You'll get plenty for this!"

IT SOUNDED LIKE SOMEBODY was snickering to theirselves as they snuck away, but I give no heed. I squinted cautiously around the big boulder, and begun sniping at the cabin. All I could see to shoot at was the puffs of smoke which marked the cracks they was shooting through, but from the cussing and yelling which begun to float up from the shack, I must have throwed some lead mighty close to them.

They kept shooting back, and the bullets splashed and buzzed on the rocks, and I kept looking at the further slope for some sign of Sheriff Hopkins and the posse. But all I heard was a sound of horses galloping away toward the west. I wondered who it could be, and I kept expecting the posse to rush down the opposite slope and take them desperadoes in the rear, and whilst I was craning my neck around a corner of the boulder--whang! A bullet smashed into the rock a few inches from my face and a sliver of stone took a notch out of my ear. I don't know of nothing that makes me madder'n to get shot in the ear.

I seen red and didn't even shoot back. A mere rifle was too paltry to satisfy me. Suddenly I realized that the big boulder in front of me was just poised on the slope, its underside partly embedded in the earth. I throwed down my rifle and bent my knees and spread my arms and gripped it.

I shook the sweat and blood outa my eyes, and bellered so them in the hollow could hear me: "I'm givin' you-all a chance to surrender! Come out, your hands up!"

They give loud and sarcastic jeers, and I yelled: "All right, you ring-tailed jackasses! If you gets squashed like a pancake, it's your own fault. Here she comes!"

And I heaved with all I had. The veins stood out on my temples, my feet sunk into the ground, but the earth bulged and cracked all around the big rock, rivelets of dirt begun to trickle down, and the big boulder groaned, give way and lurched over.

A dumfounded yell riz from the cabin. I leaped behind a bush, but the outlaws was too surprized to shoot at me. That enormous boulder was tumbling down the hill, crushing bushes flat and gathering speed as it rolled. And the cabin was right in its path.

Wild yells bust the air, the door was throwed violently open, and a man hove into view. Just as he started out of the door I let bam at him and he howled and ducked back just like anybody will when a .45-90 slug knocks their hat off. The next instant that thundering boulder hit the cabin. Smash! It knocked it sidewise like a ten pin and caved in the wall, and the whole structure collapsed in a cloud of dust and bark and splinters.

I run down the slope, and from the yells which issued from under the ruins, I knowed they hadn't all been killed.

"Does you-all surrender?" I roared.

"Yes, dern it!" they squalled. "Get us out from under this landslide!"

"Throw out yore guns," I ordered.

"How in hell can we throw anything?" they hollered wrathfully. "We're pinned down by a ton of rocks and boards and we're bein' squoze to death. Help, murder!"

"Aw, shut up," I said. "You don't hear me carryin' on in no such hysterical way, does you?"

Well, they moaned and complained, and I sot to work dragging the ruins off them, which wasn't no great task. Purty soon I seen a booted leg and I laid hold of it and dragged out the critter it was fastened to, and he looked more done up than what my brother Bill did that time he rassled a mountain lion for a bet. I took his pistol out of his belt, and laid him down on the ground and got the others out. There was three, altogether, and I disarm 'em and laid 'em out in a row.

Their clothes was nearly tore off, and they was bruised and scratched, and had splinters in their hair, but they wasn't hurt permanent. They sot up and felt of theirselves, and one of 'em said: "This here is the first earthquake I ever seen in this country."

"T'warn't no earthquake," said another'n. "It was a avalanche."

"Listen here, Joe Partland," said the first 'un, grinding his teeth, "I says it was a earthquake, and I ain't the man to be called a liar--"

"Oh, you ain't?" said the other'n, bristling up. "Well, lemme tell you somethin', Frank Jackson--"

"This ain't no time for such argyments," I admonished 'em sternly. "As for that there rock, I rolled that at you myself."

They gaped at me. "Who are you?" said one of 'em, mopping the blood offa his ear.

"Never mind," I said. "You see this here Winchester? Well, you-all set still and rest yourselves. Soon as the sheriff gets here, I'm goin' to hand you over to him."

His mouth fell open. "Sheriff?" he said, dumb-like. "What sheriff?"

"Dick Hopkins, from Grizzly Run," I said.

"Why, you derned fool!" he screamed, scrambling up.

"Set down!" I roared, shoving my rifle barrel at him, and he sank back, all white and shaking. He could hardly talk.

"Listen to me!" he gasped. "I'm Dick Hopkins! I'm sheriff of Grizzly Run! These men are my deputies."

"Yeah?" I said sarcastically. "And who was the fellows shootin' at you from the brush?"

"Tarantula Bixby and his gang," he said. "We was follerin' 'em when they jumped us, and bein' outnumbered and surprized, we took cover in that old hut. They robbed the Grizzly Run bank day before yesterday. And now they'll be gettin' further away every minute! Oh, Judas J. Iscariot! Of all the dumb, bone-headed jackasses--"

"Heh! heh! heh!" I said cynically. "You must think I ain't got no sense. If you're the sheriff, where at's your star?"

"It was on my suspenders," he said despairingly. "When you hauled me out by the laig my suspenders caught on somethin' and tore off. If you'll lemme look amongst them ruins--"

"You set still," I commanded. "You can't fool me. You're Tranchler Bixby yourself. Sheriff Hopkins told me so. Him and the posse will be here in a little while. Set still and shut up."

WE STAYED THERE, AND the fellow which claimed to be the sheriff moaned and pulled his hair and shed a few tears, and the other fellows tried to convince me they was deputies till I got tired of their gab and told 'em to shut up or I'd bend my Winchester over their heads. I wondered why Hopkins and them didn't come, and I begun to get nervous, and all to once the fellow which said he was the sheriff give a yell that startled me so I jumped and nearly shot him. He had something in his hand and was waving it around.

"See here?" His voice cracked he hollered so loud. "I found it! It must have fell down into my shirt when my suspenders busted! Look at it, you dern mountain grizzly!"

I looked and my flesh crawled. It was a shiny silver star.

"Hopkins said he lost his'n," I said weakly. "Maybe you found it in the brush."

"You know better!" he bellered. "You're one of Bixby's men. You was sent to hold us here while Tarantula and the rest made their getaway. You'll get ninety years for this!"

I turned cold all over as I remembered them horses I heard galloping. I'd been fooled! This was the sheriff! That pot-bellied thug which shot at me had been Bixby hisself! And whilst I held up the real sheriff and his posse, them outlaws was riding out of the country.

Now wasn't that a caution?

"You better gimme that gun and surrender," opined Hopkins. "Maybe if you do they won't hang you."

"Set still!" I snarled. "I'm the biggest sap that ever straddled a mustang, but even saps has their feelin's. You ain't goin' to put me behind no bars. I'm goin' up this slope, but I'll be watchin' you. I've throwed your guns over there in the brush. If any of you makes a move toward 'em, I'll put a harp in his hand."

Nobody craved a harp.

They set up a chant of hate as I backed away, but they sot still. I went up the slope backwards till I hit the rim, and then I turned and ducked into the brush and run. I heard 'em cussing somethin' awful down in the hollow, but I didn't pause. I come to where I'd left Cap'n Kidd, and a-forked him and rode, thankful them outlaws had been in too big a hurry to steal him. I throwed away the rifle they give me, and headed west.

I aimed to cross Wild River at Ghost Canyon, and head into the uninhabited mountain region beyond there. I figgered I could dodge a posse indefinite once I got there. I pushed Cap'n Kidd hard, cussing my reins which had been notched by Bixby's bullet. I didn't have time to fix 'em, and Cap'n Kidd was a iron-jawed outlaw.

He was sweating plenty when I finally hove in sight of the place I was heading for. As I topped the canyon's crest before I dipped down to the crossing, I glanced back. They was a high notch in the hills a mile or so behind me. And as I looked three horsemen was etched in that notch, against the sky behind 'em. I cussed fervently. Why hadn't I had sense enough to know Hopkins and his men was bound to have horses tied somewheres near? They'd got their mounts and follered me, figgering I'd aim for the country beyond Wild River. It was about the only place I could go.

Not wanting no running fight with no sheriff's posse, I raced recklessly down the sloping canyon wall, busted out of the bushes--and stopped short. Wild River was on the rampage--bank full in the narrow channel and boiling and foaming. Been a big rain somewhere away up on the head, and the horse wasn't never foaled which could swum it.

They wasn't but one thing to do, and I done it. I wheeled Cap'n Kidd and headed up the canyon. Five miles up the river there was another crossing, with a bridge--if it hadn't been washed away.

CAP'N KIDD HAD HIS SECOND wind and we was going lickety-split, when suddenly I heard a noise ahead of us, above the roar of the river and the thunder of his hoofs on the rocky canyon floor. We was approaching a bend in the gorge where a low ridge run out from the canyon wall, and beyond that ridge I heard guns banging. I heaved back on the reins--and both of 'em snapped in two!

Cap'n Kidd instantly clamped his teeth on the bit and bolted, like he always done when anything out of the ordinary happened. He headed straight for the bushes at the end of the ridge, and I leaned forward and tried to get hold of the bit rings with my fingers. But all I done was swerve him from his course. Instead of following the canyon bed on around the end of the ridge, he went right over the rise, which sloped on that side. It didn't slope on t'other side; it fell away abrupt. I had a fleeting glimpse of five men crouching amongst the bushes on the canyon floor with guns in their hands. They looked up--and Cap'n Kidd braced his legs and slid to a halt at the lip of the low bluff and simultaneously bogged his head and throwed me heels over head down amongst 'em.

17

My boot heel landed on somebody's head, and the spur knocked him cold and blame near scalped him. That partly bust my fall, and it was further cushioned by another fellow which I landed on in a sitting position, and which took no further interest in the proceedings. The other three fell on me with loud brutal yells, and I reached for my .45 and found to my humiliation that it had fell out of my scabbard when I was throwed.

So I riz with a rock in my hand and bounced it offa the head of a fellow which was fixing to shoot me, and he dropped his pistol and fell on top of it. At this juncture one of the survivors put a buffalo gun to his shoulder and sighted, then evidently fearing he would hit his companion which was carving at me on the other side with a bowie knife, he reversed it and run in swinging it like a club.

The man with the knife got in a slash across my ribs and I then hit him on the chin which was how his jaw-bone got broke in four places. Meanwhile the other'n swung at me with his rifle, but missed my head and broke the stock off across my shoulder. Irritated at his persistency in trying to brain me with the barrel, I laid hands on him and throwed him head-on against the bluff, which is when he got his fractured skull and concussion of the brain, I reckon.

I then shook the sweat from my eyes, and glaring down, rekernized the remains as Bixby and his gang. I might have knew they'd head for the wild Country across the river, same as me. Only place they could go.

Just then, however, a clump of bushes parted, near the river bank, and a big black-bearded man riz up from behind a dead horse. He had a six-shooter in his hand and he approached me cautiously.

"Who're you?" he demanded. "Where'd you come from?"

"I'm Breckinridge Elkins," I answered, mopping the blood offa my shirt. "What is this here business, anyway?"

"I was settin' here peaceable waitin' for the river to go down so I could cross," he said, "when up rode these yeggs and started shootin'. I'm a honest citizen--"

"You're a liar," I said with my usual diplomacy. "You're Joel Cairn, the wust outlaw in the hills. I seen your pitcher in the post office at Chawed Ear."

With that he p'inted his .45 at me and his beard bristled like the whiskers of a old timber wolf.

"So you know me, hey?" he said. "Well, what you goin' to do about it, hey? Want to colleck the reward money, hey?"

"Naw, I don't," I said. "I'm a outlaw myself, now. I just run foul of the law account of these skunks. They's a posse right behind me."

"They is?" he snarled. "Why'nt you say so? Here, le's catch these fellers' horses and light out. Cheap skates! They claims I double-crossed 'em in the matter of a stagecoach hold-up we pulled together recently. I been avoidin' 'em 'cause I'm a peaceful man by nater, but they rode onto me onexpected today. They shot my horse first crack; we been tradin' lead for more'n a hour without doin' much damage, but they'd got me eventually, I reckon. Come on. We'll pull out together."

"No, we won't," I said. "I'm a outlaw by force of circumstances, but I ain't no murderin' bandit."

"Purty particular of yore comperny, ain'tcha?" he sneered. "Well, anyways, help me catch me a horse. Yore's is still up there on that bluff. The day's still young--"

He pulled out a big gold watch and looked at it; it was one which wound with a key.

I JUMPED LIKE I WAS SHOT. "Where'd you get that watch?" I hollered.

He jerked up his head kinda startled, and said: "My grandpap gimme it. Why?"

"You're a liar!" I bellered. "You took that off'n my Uncle Garfield. Gimme that watch!"

"Are you crazy?" he yelled, going white under his whiskers. I plunged for him, seeing red, and he let bang! and I got it in the left thigh. Before he could shoot again I was on top of him, and knocked the gun up. It banged but the bullet went singing up over the bluff and Cap'n Kidd squealed and started changing ends. The pistol flew outa Cairn's hand and

20

he hit me vi'lently on the nose which made me see stars. So I hit him in the belly and he grunted and doubled up; and come up with a knife out of his boot which he cut me across the boozum with, also in the arm and shoulder and kicked me in the groin. So I swung him clear of the ground and throwed him headfirst and jumped on him with both feet. And that settled him.

I picked up the watch where it had fell, and staggered over to the cliff, spurting blood at every step like a stuck hawg.

"At last my search is at a end!" I panted. "I can go back to Ellen Reynolds who patiently awaits the return of her hero--"

It was at this instant that Cap'n Kidd, which had been stung by Cairn's wild shot and was trying to buck off his saddle, bucked hisself off the bluff. He fell on me....

The first thing I heard was bells ringing, and then they turned to horses galloping. I set up and wiped off the blood which was running into my eyes from where Cap'n Kidd's left hind hoof had split my scalp. And I seen Sheriff Hopkins, Jackson and Partland come tearing around the ridge. I tried to get up and run, but my right leg wouldn't work. I reached for my gun and it still wasn't there. I was trapped.

"Look there!" yelled Hopkins, wild-eyed. "That's Bixby on the ground--and all his gang. And ye gods, there's Joel

Cairn! What is this, anyhow? It looks like a battlefield! What's that settin' there? He's so bloody I can't recognize him!"

"It's the hill-billy!" yelped Jackson. "Don't move or I'll shoot 'cha!"

"I already been shot," I snarled. "Gwan--do yore wust. Fate is against me."

They dismounted and stared in awe.

"Count the dead, boys," said Hopkins in a still, small voice.

"Aw," said Partland, "ain't none of 'em dead, but they'll never be the same men again. Look! Bixby's comin' to! Who done this, Bixby?"

Bixby cast a wabbly eye about till he spied me, and then he moaned and shriveled up.

"He done it!" he waited. "He trailed us down like a bloodhound and jumped on us from behind! He tried to scalp me! He ain't human!" And he bust into tears.

They looked at me, and all took off their hats.

"Elkins," said Hopkins in a tone of reverence, "I see it all now. They fooled you into thinkin' they was the posse and us the outlaws, didn't they? And when you realized the truth, you hunted 'em down, didn't you? And cleaned 'em out single handed, and Joel Cairn, too, didn't you?"

"Well," I said groggily, "the truth is--"

"We understand," Hopkins soothed. "You mountain men is all modest. Hey, boys, tie up them outlaws whilst I look at Elkins' wounds."

"If you'll catch my horse," I said, "I got to be ridin' back--"

"Gee whiz, man!" he said, "you ain't in no shape to ride a horse! Do you know you got four busted ribs and a broke arm, and one leg broke and a bullet in the other'n, to say nothin' of bein' slashed to ribbons? We'll rig up a litter for you. What's that you got in your good hand?"

I suddenly remembered Uncle Garfield's watch which I'd kept clutched in a death grip. I stared at what I held in my hand; and I fell back with a low moan. All I had in my hand was a bunch of busted metal and broken wheels and springs, bent and smashed plumb beyond recognition.

"Grab him!" yelled Hopkins. "He's fainted!"

"Plant me under a pine tree, boys," I murmured weakly; "just carve on my tombstone: 'He fit a good fight but Fate dealt him the joker.'"

A FEW DAYS LATER A melancholy procession wound its way up the trail into the Humbolts. I was packed on a litter. I told 'em I wanted to see Ellen Reynolds before I died, and to show Uncle Garfield the rooins of the watch, so he'd know I done my duty as I seen it.

As we approached the locality where my home cabin stood, who should meet us but Jim Braxton, which tried to conceal his pleasure when I told him in a weak voice that I was a dying man. He was all dressed up in new buckskins and his exuberance was plumb disgustful to a man in my condition.

"Too bad," he said. "Too bad, Breckinridge. I hoped to meet you, but not like this, of course. Yore pap told me to tell you if I seen you about yore Uncle Garfield's watch. He thought I might run into you on my way to Chawed Ear to git a license--"

"Hey?" I said, pricking up my ears.

"Yeah, me and Ellen Reynolds is goin' to git married. Well, as I started to say, seems like one of them bandits which robbed the stage was a fellow whose dad was a friend of yore Uncle Garfield's back in Texas. He reckernized the name in the watch and sent it back, and it got here the day after you left--"

They say it was jealousy which made me rise up on my litter and fracture Jim Braxton's jaw-bone. I denies that. I stoops to no such petty practices. What impelled me was family conventions. I couldn't hit Uncle Garfield--I had to hit somebody--and Jim Braxton just happened to be the nearest one to me.